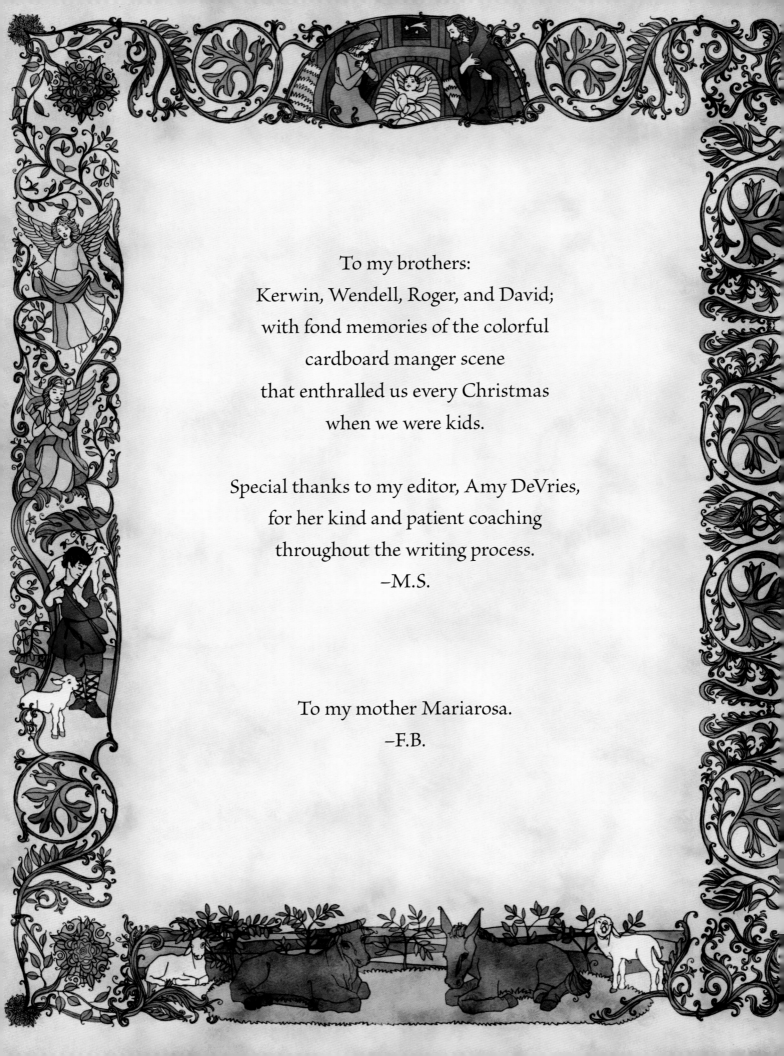

To my brothers:
Kerwin, Wendell, Roger, and David;
with fond memories of the colorful
cardboard manger scene
that enthralled us every Christmas
when we were kids.

Special thanks to my editor, Amy DeVries,
for her kind and patient coaching
throughout the writing process.
–M.S.

To my mother Mariarosa.
–F.B.

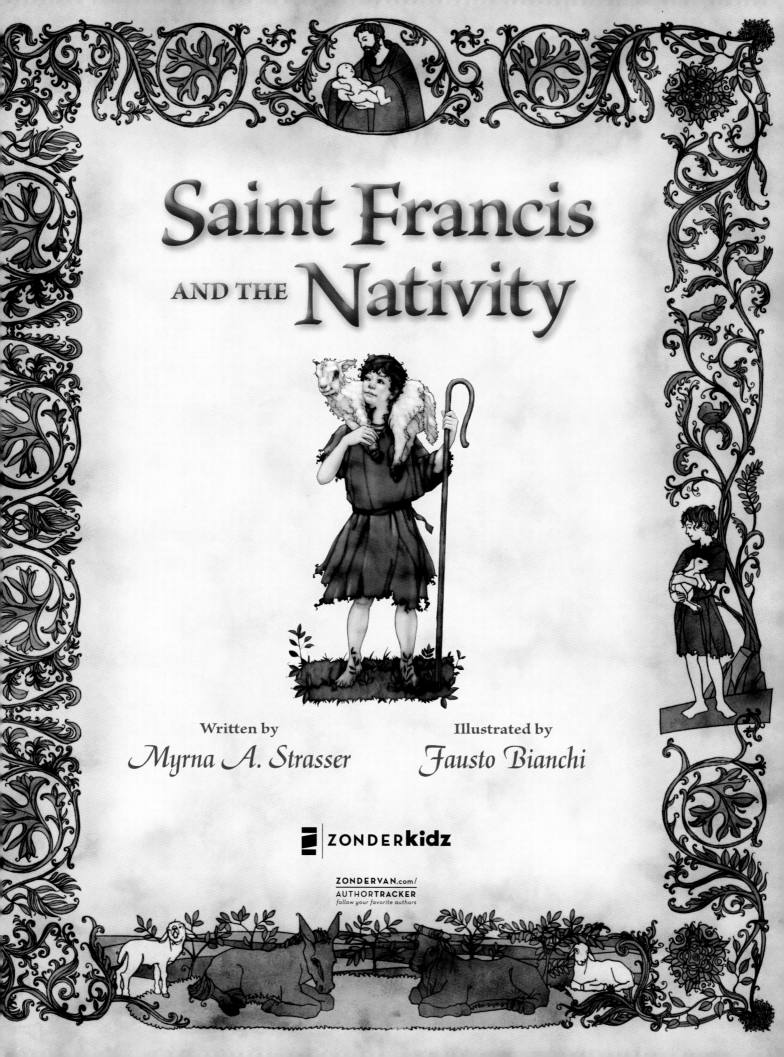

Saint Francis
AND THE Nativity

Written by
Myrna A. Strasser

Illustrated by
Fausto Bianchi

Z | ZONDERkidz

ZONDERVAN.com/
AUTHORTRACKER
follow your favorite authors

ZONDERKIDZ

Saint Francis and the Nativity
Copyright © 2010 by Myrna A. Strasser
Illustrations © 2010 by Fausto Bianchi

Requests for information should be addressed to:

Zondervan, *Grand Rapids, Michigan 49530*

Library of Congress Cataloging-in-Publication Data

Strasser, Myrna.
    St. Francis and the Nativity / by Myrna Strasser ; illustrated by Fausto Bianchi
      p.   cm.
    Summary: Tells the story of how, in 1223, St. Francis performed the first reenactment
of the birth of Jesus and introduced the traditional Christmas nativity scene.
    ISBN 978-0-310-70890-2 (hardcover)
    1. Francis, of Assisi, Saint, 1182-1226—Juvenile fiction. 2. Jesus Christ—Nativity—Juve-
nile fiction. [1. Francis, of Assisi, Saint, 1182-1226—Fiction. 2. Jesus Christ—Nativity—Fiction.
3. Saints—Fiction.] I. Bianchi, Fausto, ill. II. Title.
PZ7.S898Fi 2010
[E]—dc22
                                     200401226

All Scripture quotations, unless otherwise indicated, are taken from the Holy Bible, *New Inter-
national Version®, NIV®.* Copyright © 1973, 1978, 1984 by Biblica, Inc.™ Used by permission of
Zondervan. All rights reserved worldwide.

Any Internet addresses (websites, blogs, etc.) and telephone numbers printed in this book
are offered as a resource. They are not intended in any way to be or imply an endorsement
by Zondervan, nor does Zondervan vouch for the content of these sites and numbers for the
life of this book.

All rights reserved. No part of this publication may be reproduced, stored in a retrieval system,
or transmitted in any form or by any means—electronic, mechanical, photocopy, recording, or
any other—except for brief quotations in printed reviews, without the prior permission of the
publisher.

Zonderkidz is a trademark of Zondervan.

Editor: Amy DeVries & Barbara Herndon
Art direction & design: Kris Nelson & P.J. Lyons

Printed in China

---

10 11 12 13 14 15 / LPC / 24 23 22 21 20 19 18 17 16 15 14 13 12 11 10 9 8 7 6 5 4 3 2 1

✦ Author's Note ✦

When I was a child, as soon as the family decorated the Christmas tree, we opened the box containing the manger scene. It had a foldout base with a pop-up stable. My brothers and I would put the wise men, the shepherds, Mary and Joseph, and the baby Jesus in place. We handled each piece carefully, knowing that this represented the real meaning of Christmas.

That tradition is still honored today. In homes around the world, nativity sets are an important part of the Christmas celebration. In Italy it's called a presepio; in Spain and Latin America, a bélen; it's called a weihnachtskrippe in Germany, and a crèche in France. Whatever name we give the manger scene, we can credit Saint Francis of Assisi for the idea.

In 1223, in a mountain region in Italy, Francis and some friends performed the first live nativity display based on the description found in Luke 2. Francis insisted the reenactment be exactly like the night when Jesus was born, with only Mary and Joseph, a few animals, and no wise men.

The people who crowded into the cave for that first performance were so impressed that every year they wanted to see it again. The idea spread to other Italian towns and cities. Later, a craftsman made a miniature version of the manger scene, and the tradition spread all around Europe and eventually to America.

The popularity of the manger scene continues to this day. Whatever the depiction—with or without the wise men, a live scene with real animals, or cardboard cutouts—it's a wonderful way to celebrate the birth of Jesus.

Mario scrambled up a tall beech tree. From his perch, he could
see all of the sheep in the valley.

Mario counted each sheep. He watched them patiently and
carefully. He loved each sheep, but his favorite was Little One,
a lamb that always stayed close to Mario.

"Mario, Mr. Velita wants your help," one of the other shepherd boys called.

Mr. Giovanni Velita, the lord of the manor, was a kind man. As Mario ran toward the house, Little One followed.

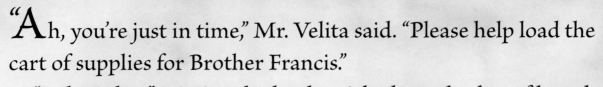

"Ah, you're just in time," Mr. Velita said. "Please help load the cart of supplies for Brother Francis."

"Who is he?" Mario asked as he picked up a basket of bread.

"Brother Francis is a good friend of mine," Mr. Velita replied. "He is a man of God, and today he is preaching in town. Why don't you come along? Sergio will watch the sheep."

When they arrived in the town of Greccio, they saw a crowd gathered in the piazza. A kind-looking man dressed in a ragged brown robe was speaking about Jesus. *He must be Brother Francis,* Mario thought.

When the robed man finished speaking, Mr. Velita introduced him.

"Hello, Mario. And who is this?" Brother Francis asked as he bent down to pet Little One.

Mario was too shy to reply to the man who drew a crowd.

"You must come and meet my animal friends sometime," Brother Francis said kindly. Mario could only smile.

After that, Mario did visit Brother Francis many times. One cool evening when Mario was helping him feed the birds, Brother Francis said, "I can see you are a good shepherd, Mario. Did you know that Jesus is a good shepherd too?"

Mario wondered what he meant. "He watches over us and guides us every day—just as you do for your sheep," his friend said softly. "But Jesus loves you even more than you love Little One."

Mario wrinkled his brow. "He does?"

"Yes," Brother Francis nodded. "More than one thousand years ago, God sent his only son, Jesus, to be born in Bethlehem.

"That night was the most important of all," Brother Francis explained. "The star that showed the way to our Savior lit up the earth."

"I wish I could have seen it," said Mario.

That night Brother Francis lay awake thinking. He wished he could show people that wondrous night in Bethlehem so many years ago. But how?

By the next day, Brother Francis had an idea—a really fantastic idea.
"We could perform a play to help people understand what happened that night," Brother Francis told Mario. "Since this is a new idea, I will need permission from the church. Mr. Velita could travel to Rome with me to ask permission."

"I will take care of your animals while you are gone," promised Mario.

"Thank you. In the meantime,"
his friend said, "we need a place for the
manger scene. Will you look for one?"
"I will try to find something," Mario said, while
he wondered where a child of God would be born.

Mario thought about Jesus the Shepherd while Brother Francis was away. When one of the sheep wandered too close to a cliff, the young shepherd gently steered it away from danger.

That's how Jesus protects me, Mario thought.

Mario and the other shepherds carefully guided their sheep to green pastures and cool streams of water.

That's how Jesus takes care of me, Mario thought.

Mario was busy every day. He watched his master's sheep. He cared for the animals that Brother Francis cared for. He thought about Brother Francis and Mr. Velita and prayed for their safe return. He hoped the church would give them permission to perform the Christmas play.

He also thought hard about where to have the manger scene. Mario knew of many possible places—the marketplace … the rolling fields … the piazza … but no place seemed special enough.

"Dear Jesus," Mario prayed, "please help me find the perfect place."

One cold, windy night, Mario couldn't find Little One. "Where are you?" he called from the beech tree. "Little One!" Mario shouted over the pastures.

Then over the rush of the wind, he heard a faint "Baa!" Mario followed the sound up a hill.

Mario was standing outside a cave when he heard Little One again. Mario ran into the cave and there was his lamb. As he scooped up Little One, Mario said a prayer of thanks to Jesus. Then he opened his eyes and saw that the cave was very large.

"Little One, you discovered the perfect place!" Mario said in a rush of joy.

A few days later, Mr. Velita and Brother Francis returned from Rome. "Good news, Mario!" Mr. Velita said. "We received permission to have the Christmas play."

"Hooray!" cried Mario. "And I found the perfect place to hold it. Come with me!"

When they arrived at the cave, Brother Francis looked at Mario with sparkling eyes. "This spot is simple and humble, but it feels as if something important could take place here. It's perfect."

Mr. Velita left to get started on the play right away. Over the next few days, clean straw and animals were brought to the cave.

At last Christmas Eve arrived. The ox, the donkey, and the empty manger were all in the cave. The only one missing was baby Jesus.

With torches and candles to light their way, townspeople traveled slowly up the mountain. Their voices echoed through the wide valley.

Mario and Brother Francis watched and waited on the hilltop with beaming faces. "Here they come!" Mario shouted.

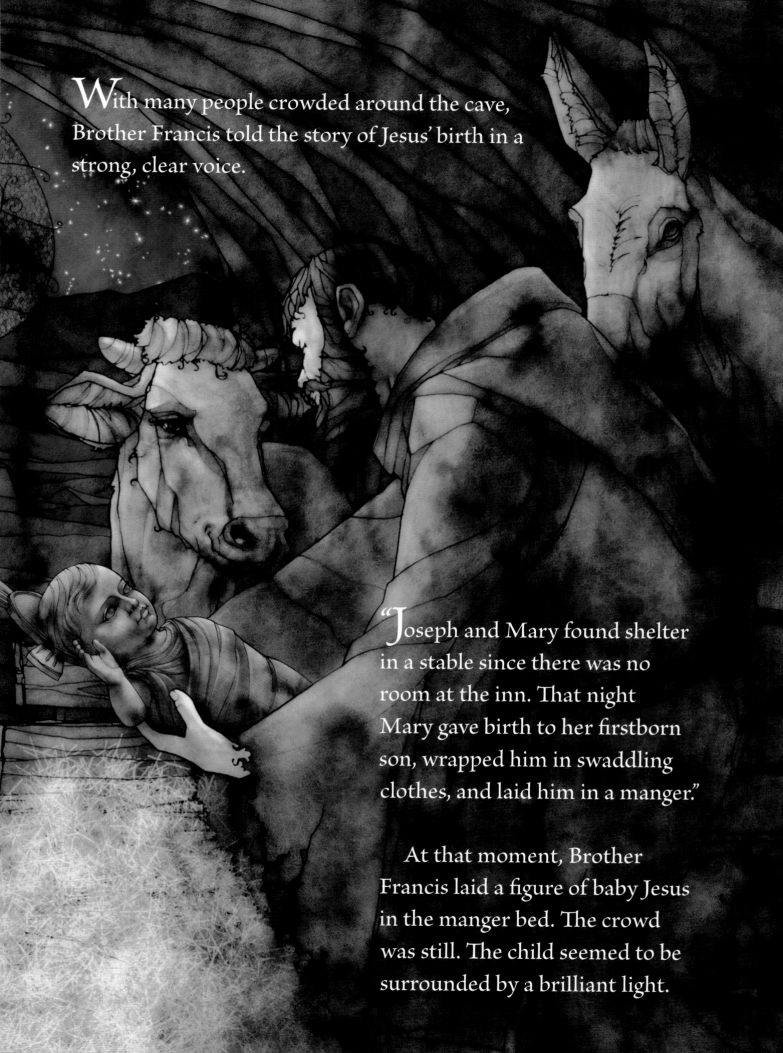

With many people crowded around the cave, Brother Francis told the story of Jesus' birth in a strong, clear voice.

"Joseph and Mary found shelter in a stable since there was no room at the inn. That night Mary gave birth to her firstborn son, wrapped him in swaddling clothes, and laid him in a manger."

At that moment, Brother Francis laid a figure of baby Jesus in the manger bed. The crowd was still. The child seemed to be surrounded by a brilliant light.

Throughout the night, hundreds of lights moved up and down the mountain, as people "came to adore him." When they discovered the nativity scene with real animals, the birth of Christ seemed to happen before them.

Mario finally caught the eye of Brother Francis, and the two friends exchanged smiles. This truly had been an amazing night.

Then Mario bowed his head. "Thank you, dear Jesus, for coming to be our Savior and our Good Shepherd," he whispered.

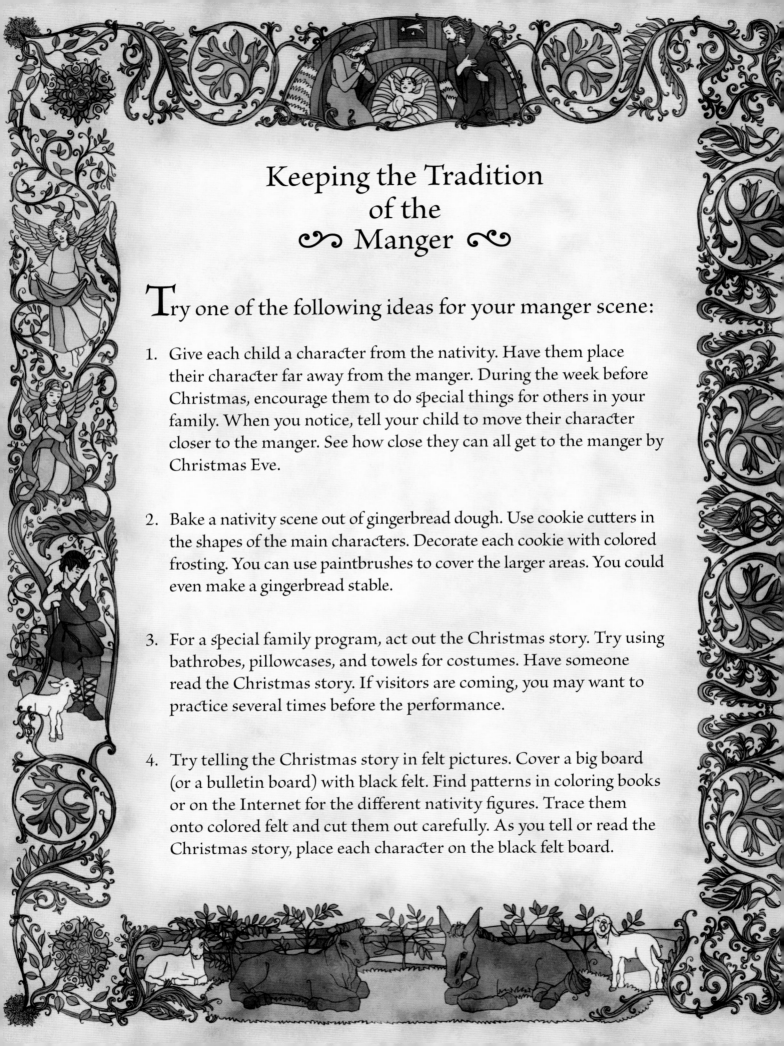

Keeping the Tradition
of the
ᴥ Manger ᴥ

Try one of the following ideas for your manger scene:

1. Give each child a character from the nativity. Have them place their character far away from the manger. During the week before Christmas, encourage them to do special things for others in your family. When you notice, tell your child to move their character closer to the manger. See how close they can all get to the manger by Christmas Eve.

2. Bake a nativity scene out of gingerbread dough. Use cookie cutters in the shapes of the main characters. Decorate each cookie with colored frosting. You can use paintbrushes to cover the larger areas. You could even make a gingerbread stable.

3. For a special family program, act out the Christmas story. Try using bathrobes, pillowcases, and towels for costumes. Have someone read the Christmas story. If visitors are coming, you may want to practice several times before the performance.

4. Try telling the Christmas story in felt pictures. Cover a big board (or a bulletin board) with black felt. Find patterns in coloring books or on the Internet for the different nativity figures. Trace them onto colored felt and cut them out carefully. As you tell or read the Christmas story, place each character on the black felt board.

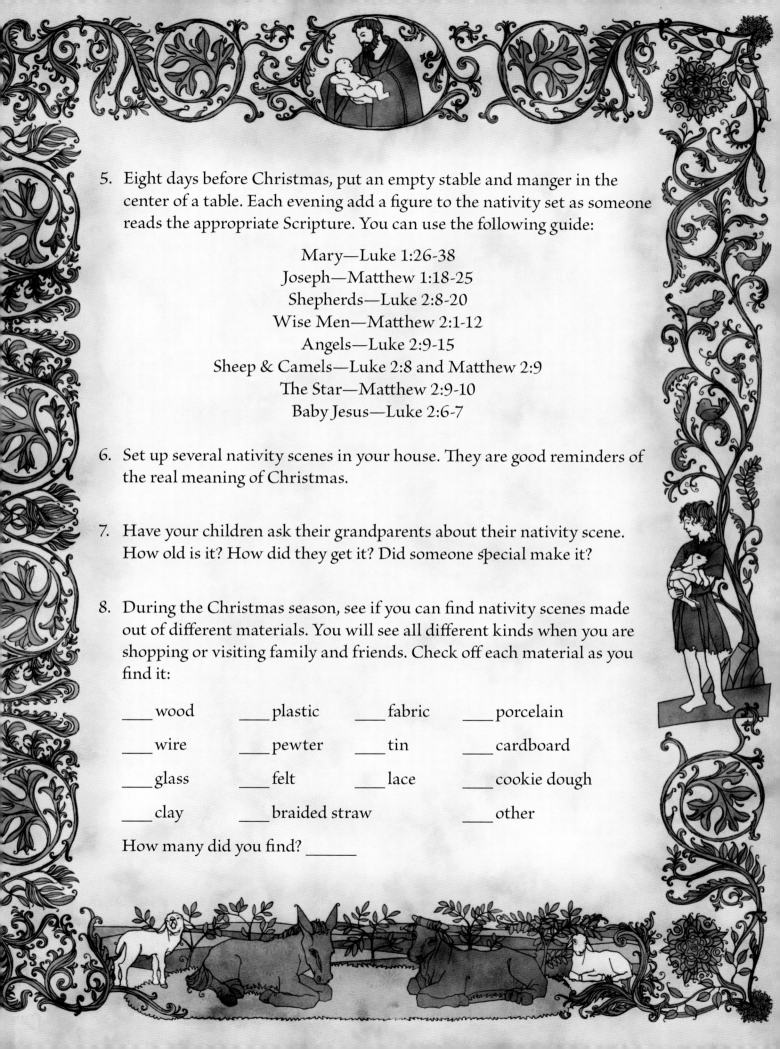

5. Eight days before Christmas, put an empty stable and manger in the center of a table. Each evening add a figure to the nativity set as someone reads the appropriate Scripture. You can use the following guide:

Mary—Luke 1:26-38
Joseph—Matthew 1:18-25
Shepherds—Luke 2:8-20
Wise Men—Matthew 2:1-12
Angels—Luke 2:9-15
Sheep & Camels—Luke 2:8 and Matthew 2:9
The Star—Matthew 2:9-10
Baby Jesus—Luke 2:6-7

6. Set up several nativity scenes in your house. They are good reminders of the real meaning of Christmas.

7. Have your children ask their grandparents about their nativity scene. How old is it? How did they get it? Did someone special make it?

8. During the Christmas season, see if you can find nativity scenes made out of different materials. You will see all different kinds when you are shopping or visiting family and friends. Check off each material as you find it:

____ wood	____ plastic	____ fabric	____ porcelain
____ wire	____ pewter	____ tin	____ cardboard
____ glass	____ felt	____ lace	____ cookie dough
____ clay	____ braided straw		____ other

How many did you find? _____